LEGENDS IN BRASS

VOLUME 1

JAMES SHEPHERD

The Famous Newbiggin-by-the-Sea Cornet Player

(Died June 2023)

Christopher D. Helme B.E.M

Published by: Mews Publishing (Lightcliffe), Halifax HX3 8TY
ISBN: 0 9536705 0 3

ACKNOWLEDGEMENTS

I would like to thank the following people for all the help and encouragement they have given me during the preparation of this story about one of the brass band movement's finest ambassadors.

Ralph Lowery – former Eb flat Bass with Grimethorpe Colliery Band and a long time family friend; Geoffrey Whitham – another long standing family friend, conductor, adjudicator and former principal Euphonium and Resident Conductor Black Dyke Mills Band. John Clay – former Cornet and Flugel Horn Black Dyke Mills Band, conductor; David Horsfield – former Cornet player Brighouse and Rastrick Band, Black Dyke Mills Band, original member James Shepherd Versatile Brass, conductor, adjudicator, music publisher and recording company. Barry Thompson – former Carlton Main and Frickley Colliery Band, Grimethorpe Colliery Band, conductor, teacher and adjudicator.

Ronald Helme for his proof reading skills; Dennis Hussey (photographer – photograph page 36), Philip Chisholm (Studio Tristan Photography, photographs page 1& 34), Chris Freeman (photographer) and all those friends and fellow professional musicians who have all gladly given their help and tributes. All who have both known and/or worked with James Shepherd over the last fifty years. These tributes can be found at the back of this publication.

A number of images in this publication were obtained from IMSI's Master Clip/Master Photos © Collection, 1895, Francisco Blvd, East, San Rafael, CA 94901-5506,USA

...and finally ....Jim Shepherd for his help and co-operation in preparing this publication and the loan of many family photographs.

INTRODUCTION

Those within the brass band world are often heard to boast that the movement has a long history. Listening to the reminiscences from some of the older retired bandsmen conjures up images of a far different movement than we have today.

Following the many changes over the last fifty years particularly with social and working practices the brass band movement has seen many of its household name bands fade and disappear. Inevitably with the passage of time many of the former players from those bands, particularly the ones that old men would debate over in contest tea rooms as to just who was the best player there ever was, sadly they have also gone or retired into almost obscurity as well.

If you are lucky you can still find a few old scratchy 78rpm records in the antique or second hand shops or flea markets of some of the truly great players from the past. Such famous names as Arthur Laycock, Edwin Firth, Jack Mackintosh, Harold Moss and Harry Mortimer. Even now in more recent times whilst looking through the charity shop record boxes you can usually find plenty of discarded brass bands LP's. If you look hard enough just now and then you will find one which has a solo by Derek Garside, Bert Sullivan, Ken Smith, Trevor Groom or Maurice Murphy and of course Jim Shepherd.

It was after a discussion with a young friend a few years ago that I realised he had never heard of many of these fine musicians. Performers who could only be described as legends within the movement highlighted to me and posed the question:

'...where is the written history about these past masters, now all their old records are becoming unplayable or their CD's have been deleted..?'

It is for that reason I have compiled this first publication, a thumbnail sketch telling the story of one of the finest cornet players this country has ever produced. Someone whose contribution to teaching within the brass band movement is practically unrivalled in the modern era. The tributes at the end of the story are testament that now after fifty years he is justifiably considered to be a legend within the brass band movement.

LEGENDS IN BRASS

JAMES SHEPHERD

The Famous Newbiggin-by-the-Sea Cornet Player

James Shepherd - 1997

Visiting my grandparents' home on a Saturday was something I did quite often as a boy, something that I considered a regular treat. Fish and chip dinners, the extra sweet rations and a little less discipline than at my own home and perhaps half-a-crown from Grandad to go to the Saturday morning pictures - those were the days.

The highlight of the day however, was none of those nor any of the usual treats that most children craved for - but a peek inside Grandma's old tin box she kept tucked away in the cellar. Whether it was the history and nostalgia that her old brown rusty tin box contained that gave me my own interest of delving into the past I can only surmise.

This old brown tin box contained a life time of memories, the deeper I dug into the mass of old papers and faded sepia photographs the further I delved in time.

Looking back now as I sat there removing each layer of time from my Grandma and Grandad's life. I feel it was almost like some prying archaeologist and it has often gone through my mind since then that you must be old to have had a box like that in the first place.

As a young cornet player in those now far off days, I too like many others entered the usual round of Slow Melody competitions. Never winning, but as always and not to be disillusioned altogether after noting the judge's written remarks, which more often than not suggested that with a little more practice I could do better.

I stuck the judges comments which to anybody else would be nothing more now than a few scraps of paper, onto pieces of card cut from old Cornflake packets and along with old concert and contest programmes, newspapers cuttings, letters and many other items of juvenile memorabilia I carefully put them together in an old shoe box - that's almost forty years ago now.

Recently having cleared and boarded the loft out at home I took my young son up into the loft to help sort out a few odds and ends.

"What's in this box Dad ?" , he said with a tone of curiosity in his voice. It was something I'd kept over the years but in recent years was something I'd completely forgotten about. Looking through the box's contents those childhood visits to my Grandparents home came flooding back and then I suddenly realised - this was my old tin box - ....did I now qualify to being old and nostalgic. ?

Looking through the old programmes they brought back memories of me struggling to master the third cornet parts in the Clifton and Lightcliffe Band, a fourth section band in the late 1950's and early 1960's, a job that I recall was no easy task.

Amongst the old papers there were some memorable magical moments that I will never forget. There was a letter which when originally written I imagined had been on rather nice blue writing paper, but as the years have gone by, it had become soiled and faded.

The letter was dated June 28th 1966 and was from a Mr J. Shepherd of 5 Inghead Cottages, Queensbury - asking if I could possibly go along to help his Saturday morning Music Centre band at Brooksbank School, Victoria Road, Elland.

Still struggling and I suppose could have done better, I still however enjoy playing the Eb Bass, these days with the West Yorkshire Police Band after yet another spell with the Clifton and Lightcliffe Band and the Elland Silver Band. It has been during the years with the Police band that we accompanied the same Mr James Shepherd on a number of guest appearances he did with the band. Looking back thirty odd years to those far off days at Elland and that letter - a request from my and many other young cornet players hero - just imagine being asked to go and play with his band, something savoured and never to be forgotten.

James Shepherd ....but who is this man, someone who has given so much to the brass band movement for half a century.

He grew up in the North of England and with the encouragement of his father he began playing the cornet alongside other youngsters in his local band at Newbiggin-by-the-Sea. Over the next twenty years his dedication to both practice and the determination to succeed was to eventually see him achieving the pinnacle of every young cornet players ambitions with his appointment as the principal cornet player for the world famous Black Dyke Mills Band.

A cornet player who was to follow in the footsteps of such legendary cornet players as Ceres Jackson, who had sat in the same top chair some fifty years earlier, Harold Jackson, Owen Bottomley, Willie Lang and Maurice Murphy, players who had also led the band with the highest distinction. To go on and sit in the same chair as those select few famous and distinguished cornet players and lead them to unrivalled success would ensure his place in being regarded, in the eyes of many people, as one of the brass band movement's true Legends.

James (Jim) Shepherd was the youngest of two children and was born on November 25th, 1936 the only son of James and Florence Shepherd, a couple who were better known to their many friends in their small close knit community as Dickie and Florrie. Along with his parents Jim and his elder sister Florence who, like her mother was known to her friends and relatives as Florrie lived and grew up at 42, Westmorland Avenue in the North Eastern coastal town of Newbiggin-by-the-Sea, Northumberland.

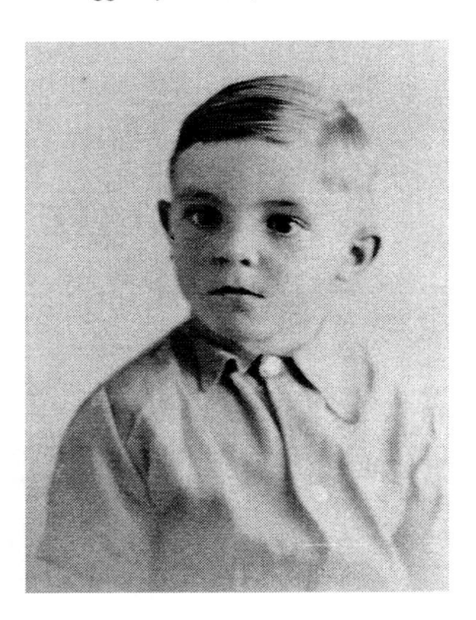

Young James Shepherd - brought up in a musical household

Brass music in the Shepherd household was an every day sound through his father being a noted local cornet and trumpet player, in addition to being a renowned tenor saxaphone player in the local community. He was a man who in his younger days had received a number of offers to move away to join other bands but he always resisted the temptation to leave his native Newbiggin-by-the-Sea. In later years he did break with his traditional music making by joining a number of local dance bands who were in regular demand at many a local 'Hop' in and around Newbiggin. In 1961 he was appointed the new conductor of the Newbiggin and Lynmouth Band - indeed a man of many parts.

'Dickie' Shepherd - (front left) was a noted Cornet, Trumpet and Tenor Saxophone player

'Dickie' Shepherd died in 1991 aged 84 years and as a tribute a recording of Jim performing an arrangement of 'The Lords Prayer' was played at his funeral. His mother Florence passed away in June 1998.

Just as the other local youngsters in his community he attended the Newbiggin Infant's School and then moved up to the Newbiggin Colliery Junior School and then at the age of eleven he moved to West End Modern School at Newbiggin where he was selected to play for the school football team.

The Newbiggin West End Modern School football team of 1950,

Jim Shepherd is the one kneeling on the front right side

His school days came to end at the age of fifteen when he left to start work in the grocery department at the local Co-op.

Young Jim was just like all the other Newbiggin lads, up to a little mischief now and then. He had his secrets too, which I suppose we all had when we were kids. One of Jim's special secrets was the time he kept a spider in a toilet as a pet. No one and I mean no one was allowed near it and any sign of the spider's web being brushed aside and there was hell to play. Not only did he protect the spider's web but also he fed it on freshly trapped fly's as well....the things we did as kids.

Taking up a brass instrument was seen as the natural order of things in the Shepherd household so when his father introduced him to the cornet on his thirteenth birthday and began giving him lessons it came as little surprise.

Under his father's wing he went along to the local Newbiggin Colliery Band rehearsal room where he was encouraged to sit in with the other youngsters in a Junior Band they had started. It wasn't long however before he was recognised as a promising third cornet player and it was on this first visit that he was introduced to the senior band's bandmaster George Wright. This man was to be an inspiration to him in those formative years as a young cornet player and someone who Jim still speaks highly of even now after all these years.

Jim aged 13 years standing between two friends of the family who were visiting from Edinburgh.

One of his first ventures as a soloist was at the local Salvation Army Citadel where they held entertainment evenings where local youngsters were invited along to take part and show what they could do.

It was on one of these occasions that as a guest player that Jim stepped forward and performed that well loved standard for all beginners, 'Bless This House'. In later years his first private tutor after his father was Billy Lidster the Euphonium player at the North Seaton Band. Now under the wing of Billy Lidster it wasn't long after these early performances that Jim was beginning to be noticed at these musical evenings and local slow melody competitions.

Having listened to him live, on countless records and C.D.'s over many years I can't believe it could ever be considered or suggested that he might have ever suffered with nerves before a performance. However, one story from his childhood days which illustrates there is no shame in being nervous was before one particular solo competition at the North Seaton Band contest. It has been said that he was so nervous that he visited the local church and prayed - obviously someone was listening that day because he played so well that he won the first prize.

In 1954 his time had come to do National Service, his two years were spent as the principal cornet player in the Royal Army Medical Corps Staff Band at Aldershot under the direction of Lt Col Louis Brown M.D. Having completed his two years he stayed on in the regulars for another year concentrating exclusively on his music and musical performance. This gave him the opportunity of practising the famous cornet tutor book of Jean Baptiste Arban day after day throughout his three years service. Jim's father had been a miner and was determined that his son would not follow the same path for his future employment. Within three months at Aldershot he was appointed the band's principal solo cornet player taking over what in band circles was a 'red lip player', someone whose lips couldn't last long. This gave Jim the chance to work at his technique and develop his recognised potential even further.

October 1954 and Jim shows off his new uniform

Looking back now those who have had the opportunity of listening to him playing live or on a recording can now appreciate just how those hours of practice have given him such a renowned reputation for his articulation and technical brilliance.

On his return home in 1957 his reputation as a cornet player was beginning to spread and was being considered by many as the rising star. This new found local fame saw him leave the Newbiggin Band following an invitation to join the Pegswood Band as their principal cornet, a band he still remembers as being very enthusiastic and socially one of the best bands he was to be involved with. In March 1960 he entered the Northumberland League Solo and quartet contest, just one of the many senior solo competitions he was to take part in over the next few years.

On that day he played an arrangement of Chopin's 'Nocturne' and was awarded the Senior Soloist winners prize, a result that he was to be become quite accustom to.

A proud moment for the Shepherd family was on Friday 9th December 1960 when father and son Jimmy and James jnr, played the trumpet obligato in 'The Trumpet shall sound' from the Messiah at a performance of the oratorio at Ashington Methodist Church.

Father and son before they performed the trumpet obligato 'The Trumpet shall sound' from the Messiah at a performance of the oratorio at Ashington Methodist Church in 1960.

On his return from National Service he like many other young men returning to civvy street had to make a living some how. Looking back now it's a long way from working at the Newbiggin Co-op Grocery Department which had been his job since leaving school to appearing and performing in some of the largest concert halls in the world.

In the banding world just as in the world of football there are certain individuals who are known as 'Talent Scouts' or 'Spotters'. One of those was family friend Ralph Lowery who in 1960 strongly recommended Jim to Jack Atherton (1909-1983), a giant in the banding world at that time. Jack Atherton had seen the best, he was at Harton Colliery where he had Norman Ashcroft and Maurice Murphy and at the C.W.S.(Manchester) Band where he had the legendary Derek Garside.

Having sent the word to Jack Atherton about this new and promising cornet player it was whilst Carlton were on their way back from the Edinburgh Festival Invitation Contest that Jack Atherton called unannounced into the Co-op and basically gave Jim two choices ....*'stay in Newbiggin and be a grocer or come down to Yorkshire and get into the business of banding'*......... these words were enough to persuade Jim to go south and join Carlton as their new principal cornet.

Jack Atherton was the conductor of the Carlton Main and Frickley Colliery Band, a band that was riding high back in those days. Although he led them to victory at the British Open in 1958 on Eric Ball's 'Sunset Rhapsody' and at many of the C.I.S.W.O. Contests in Blackpool they were never to win the national title but like many others came very close. Their run of success began in 1957 with a 3rd place, they were unplaced in 1958, 2nd in 1959 to Black Dyke in one of the most memorable finals, playing Frank Wright's arrangement of Lalo's 'Le Roi d'Y's'. In 1960 playing Herbert Howells 'Three Figures' once again they were awarded second place only this time it was behind Stanley Boddington and the Munn and Felton's Band.

It was on the back of this success that Jim was 'spotted'. Ralph Lowery had such a respected reputation for spotting the potential rising stars that Jack Atherton signed Jim on as the band's principal cornet player without even hearing him perform. Ironically after Jim was signed Carlton did not appear at the London finals again until 1971 then under the baton of Robert Oughton. On that occasion although playing 'Le Roi d'Y's' once again on that day they were unplaced.

If Jim's nerves were ever to be exposed this first rehearsal at Carlton was likely to be the day. He took the rehearsal by *storm*, it was said at the time that some doubted Jack Atherton's wisdom in signing players untested but they were soon left speechless once they heard the brilliance of his performance. Over the last fifty years these have not been the only musicians who have sat back listening, wishing and no doubt thinking if only I 'd kept the practice up ......

On that first visit he was asked to play a solo, he chose to play William Rimmer's 'Hailstorm', his technical ability, a quality that has stayed with him throughout his career, left everyone in the bandroom in no doubt at all that Jack Atherton had found a gem.

Living away from his hometown of Newbiggin was a new experience even for a lad of twenty-four back in those days. To make life easy and no doubt acting as his minder and the ever watchful eye on behalf of his mother he stayed with Mr and Mrs Ralph Lowery who he knew as Aunty and Uncle. Although not blood relatives the Shepherds and Lowerys had been long standing neighbours back in the 'residential' area of Newbiggin.

During the four years he stayed with Carlton he saw major success and was soon accepted both by the band and their followers. It has been written that Bill Sykes who in 1954 as the Colliery Manager became Chairman of the band and just like the new chairman of a football club he had big ideas and high expectations for his band. It was he who brought in Jack Atherton as the driving force that would turn the band into a force to be reckoned with. It has been said that it was Bill Sykes who first heard Jim Shepherd play and after seeing his parents he was the first player signed up by Bill Sykes and Jack Atherton.

On December 11th, 1960 one of his first public outings in and around the community was at the South Elmsall Welfare where he proved very popular with the audience when along with Frank and Bill Wessen who performed a trombone feature he left the audience spell bound with his artistry.

At the celebrated Edinburgh Festival Invitation Contest he led Carlton to first place playing Grenville Bantock's test piece 'The Frogs of Aristophane', even with Jack Atherton conducting to win as they did playing off number one was no easy task. It was Jim that made the difference and had given them the edge over all other bands taking part that day - he alone would always be worth one or two extra points to any top-flight band he joined.

The three years from 1962 to 1964 will go down in Jim's banding career as the turning point when he was to rise from being a good player to becoming one of the great players and on the first rungs of the ladder to becoming the brass band legend he is today.

It all began in 1962 when he was awarded the coveted first place as the Champion Soloist of Great Britain playing William Rimmer's 'Carnival of Venice'.

To win it once is a dream for most people but Jim went on to win not just a second time in 1963 playing the same piece but achieved the unique hat trick of wins in 1964.

Jim receives the Champion Cornet Soloist trophy for a unique third time in 1964

The position .of Principal Cornet at Black Dyke Mills Band became vacant following the move by Maurice Murphy to join the BBC Northern Symphony Orchestra as the Principal Trumpet player in the February of 1962.

This created a serious problem for Black Dyke Mills - who could they get to step into the shoes of another man who was to become a brass band legend ?.

For at least one broadcast and a concert at Stalybridge John Clay had been moved from second cornet to take the second man spot but was then promoted from that position to the Principal Cornet for those two engagements. However, after the Stalybridge engagement a decision was taken that through John's inexperience Maurice Murphy's number two David Pratt should be moved up to fill in for the time being, a decision that John Clay was happy with.

The London Finals were held on Saturday October 20th of that year and although David Pratt led the band under the baton of Leighton Lucas (who was to not only compose film music such as 'Ice Cold in Alex' but a composition that went on to be the 1999 National Brass Band Championships second section area test piece 'A Symphonic Suite) and although playing off number three they were not in the prizes but saw what was to be a popular victory for Alex Mortimer and his C.W.S.(Manchester) Band.

The following year was a rare event with Black Dyke Mills not qualifying at the area contest. The area test piece at Bradford in 1963 was Wagner's 'Rienzi' and as a temporary measure Black Dyke Mills were led by their guest Principal Cornet, New Zealand born Keith Caldwell and former second man to Derek Garside at C.W.S. (Manchester) Band. They could only manage fourth place behind the eventual winners Grimethorpe Colliery Band who were conducted by George Thompson.

The Bradford area contest for 1963 will be remembered for another and more serious incident when their conductor George Hespe (1900-1979) suffered a heart attack on stage and although he managed to finish the piece he never went to London again.

In April of 1963 Jim was invited to be the guest Principal Cornet at Black Dyke's summer engagement at Cliffe Castle, Keighley. At the conclusion of the concert he was heard to say that he felt the band had such a big sound they were far too strong for him. He doubted whether he was really good enough not only to join but also to lead this world famous band - sentiments that most of the principal cornet players to perform with Black Dyke have echoed.

With a little bit of persuasion he was eventually convinced that with a little time and patience the band would work with him. It took three months for both Jim and the band to settle in to each other.

Being invited to join a top band many wouldn't need asking twice but Jim overcame his initial reluctance after two of the band's big guns in the form of Jack Emmott and Geoff Whitham visited him at his home in Newbiggin-by-the-Sea and they were determined to get the best man for the job.

Black Dyke Mills Band 1966 with their Musical Director Mr Geoffrey Whitham

Back Row (left to right): Jack Brook, John Savage, Stephen Thornton, Eric Bland, William Gibson, John Clay, Len Haley (percussion), Sam Smith.
Middle Row: Brian Wood, Wally Shaw, Gordon Sutcliffe, James Shepherd, David Pratt. Frank Berry, David Summersgill, Derek Southcott
Front Row: Peter McNab, Charlie Emmott, John Clough, John Slinger, Geoffrey Whitham, Colin Hardy, Brian Broadbent, Ernest Keaton, Derek Jackson.

Looking back now this initial reluctance although not intential was probably a good move - who could have followed the legendary Maurice Murphy....?, following the band's uncharacteristic performance by their own standards in not qualifying for the 1963 London Finals.

Jim did of course finally join the band after eight months of persuasion and soul searching as to whether he could meet the bands much acclaimed and renowned high standards. He went on to lead them from that disappointment to unprecedented success over the next decade.

The move from Carlton to Black Dyke came in April / May 1963 and was a move that once again had been actively encouraged by Ralph Lowery.

Moving into a new area he had of course to make a living and find some kind of full time employment. He had been working with youngsters for some time and this was a role he enjoyed and seemed the most likely area to look into, hoping he could join the many other well known brass band instrumentalists and conductors as a peripatetic music teacher.

It was at the end of 1963 that he and Geoff Whitham, someone who was to become a life long friend, arrived at 'The Manor House', in Brighouse for an interview with the West Riding Education Authority for the vacant positions of a full time and a part time peripatetic music teacher.

Working every Saturday morning was not a commitment that Geoff was able to give and whilst he was the more likely of the two to be offered the full time position. However, owing to this problem it was Jim who was subsequently offered the full time post and Geoff the part time job a decision that in the end suited them both.

Jim took to his new job like a duck to water and it was in this new role that he began his Saturday morning brass classes at Brooksbank School in Elland and where I was to meet him two years later after receiving his invitation to join his school band.

The National Youth Brass Band Easter course of 1965 in Huddersfield saw him being invited to become a cornet tutor as a replacement for Jack Emmott the former bandmaster at Black Dyke.

The number of youngsters waiting to join the Queensbury Music Centre was growing at such a rate that all those between the ages of 8 and 12 were invited to form a junior band under Jim's guiding hand. This photograph was taken on the 21st May 1971

Following the demise of the Black Dyke Junior Band in 1967 an approach was made by Jim to Mr Peter Lambert who was not only the senior band's President but was also on the main Board of Directors at John Foster's Black Dyke Mills.

He asked him if he could use the instruments on a loan basis from the now defunct Black Dyke Juniors to teach children at Queensbury Schools.

In 1969 Jim formed the Queensbury Music Centre as part of his teaching role with the West Riding Education Committee. In the beginning he was still the principal cornet player at Black Dyke Mills and had to share his time between the band and his employers. He began by inviting children from as young as eight years old to his Saturday morning rehearsals.

Little did he realise at this time that these young people were destined to take the brass band movement by storm. Practically straight away he entered them into the Yorkshire area qualification contest of the newly formed youth section of the National Brass Band Championships.

At their very first attempt playing Eric Ball's test piece 'In Switzerland' on Saturday October 11th 1969 playing under the name of Queensbury Schools Youth Band and conducted by Jack Haigh they were awarded 194 points to win and become the National Youth Champions of Great Britain.

Further success came when they were awarded a third prize the following year and then went on to repeat their 1969 success by becoming champions again in 1971 and then to take second place in 1972.

This was certainly a hectic time in Jim's life and not all through his band commitments either, the most important date being on August 26th 1967 when he and his fiancée Anne Carpenter were married at Cross Gates Methodist Church in Leeds.

This meant both he and Black Dyke had to miss that year's British Open Championship at Belle Vue, Manchester.

In 1970 he took his young band on to the Tees-side International Eisteddfod where they won first prize and were runners up two years later. The following year they were the runners up in the British Youth Brass Band Championships at Liverpool.

Gradually the reputation and success of the band created a situation where more and more youngsters were wanting to join this high quality music centre - not only was it the name and reputation of James Shepherd that attracted them but the band's success was becoming a magnet to many young brass instrumentalists.

The number of youngsters joining and wanting to join were growing at such a rate that all those youngsters between 8 and 12 years of age formed the junior band under the guidance of Jim and the older members between the ages of 12 and 17 years became the senior band and were under the guidance and baton of Andrew Owenson.

Taking part in foreign trips, tours and exchanges are nothing new in the brass band world, Black Dyke Mills Band visited Canada at the turn of the century and again in 1972 and countless other far away and on occasions exotic locations. In 1973 and again in 1974 the Queensbury Music Centre's senior band took part in exchange visits with a youth band from Gothenburg, Sweden. The following year their exchange visit brought them a little nearer home with a trip to Selkirk in Scotland.

Shortly after that success and almost before the applause had died down and was still ringing in their ears, unknown to them changes and decisions were taking place in local authority circles that were to initially have a devastating affect on the band.

In 1974 Queensbury had become part of the Bradford Metropolitan Borough area and the authorities were of the opinion that the pressures brought on by entering contests were far too much for one of their Further Education Classes and in July 1976 ordered them to stop.

The effect on the band caused the Queensbury Music Centre Band to break away and become an independent band conducted by Andrew Owensen. The council's decision shocked everyone from band members to the committee and probably non-more so than the dedicated parents of the youngsters involved.

Above all the news came as a devastating blow to both Jim and Andrew Owenson particularly after their hard work and dedication bringing unprecedented successes, which had, culminated in their qualification to participate in the 1976 London Finals.

The band's ever growing reputation in the contest field that kept them at the forefront of the band press. In March 1975 they took first place at the Oldham Metropolitan Borough Brass Band Championships only this time they had left the ranks of youth bands to take on the fourth section bands, many of which were predominantly made up of adults.

Having swept everyone aside at Oldham they then went on to the Trans-Pennine Challenge Contest where they were awarded a creditable second prize. The real test came in February 1976 at St George's Hall in Bradford when they entered the fourth section of the Yorkshire Area of the National Brass Band contest. Although they did not win their section, for the first time they had now qualified to play at the National Brass Band Championship Finals in London.

On Saturday October 9th, at Hammersmith Town Hall under the baton of their conductor Andrew Owensen and playing off number five they played Albert Jakeway's test piece 'A Czech Fantasy' and romped home first with 184 points to become National Fourth Section Champions of Great Britain for 1976.

They returned home to Queensbury the following day to the type of Civic Reception usually reserved for Black Dyke but on this occasion the village of Queensbury had a double celebration with Black Dyke having become national champions once again as well.

Within a month Queensbury were on the winning trail once again when they were runners up back at the Oldham contest and winners of the Calderdale Youth Band Festival. In 1977 they were in the prizes at the spring contest at the Belle Vue Festival firstly with a 2nd prize in the Senior Cup and then going on to take the 1st prize the following year.

In 1978 on the 'Look Record' label they produced a long playing record with the Castleford Male Voice Choir which they titled appropriately 'Yorkshire Mixture'.

Over the next few years in the contesting field the band went from strength to strength; 1981: Yorkshire Youth Section, placed 2nd - 1982: Yorkshire 4th Section, placed 2nd - 1983: Yorkshire 4th Section, Champions - 1984: Yorkshire 3rd Section, Champions - 1985: Yorkshire 3rd Section, Champions.

These successes culminated in 1986 with the band taking first prize in the second section of the National Brass Band Championship's in London a result that gave them automatic qualification to join the Yorkshire Area Championship Section. It is widely acknowledged that the Yorkshire Championship section is arguably the most difficult section to qualify from for the London Finals - 1987: Yorkshire Championship Section placed 7th.

Without doubt the band's greatest triumph, although they neither qualified nor won a prize, many would say came in 1988 when they were awarded a creditable fourth prize in the Yorkshire Area contest which was two places above their prestigious neighbours Black Dyke Mills.

It was certainly true to say that from those early Saturday morning rehearsals Jim Shepherd had taken a group of young musicians and turned them into a first class team.
He had created an atmosphere amongst the band's members that they all seriously believed and knew the band was destined to go much further even though they were no longer under his direction.

Today the Queensbury Band is an ungraded band but still gives an opportunity to youngsters to make music. With the involvement of Jim's former colleague and old friend from Black Dyke, cornet player Fred Ellis, these youngsters will certainly benefit from his knowledge and experience.

1986 - another successful year for the Jayess Queensbury Band

The local authority being Jim's employer had left him in a very difficult position with no option but to start all over again from scratch - this saw the birth of his new band at the South Bradford Music Centre in the summer of 1976.

It was widely known he was a hard taskmaster and would rarely tolerate absentees, even so there was still countless young players queuing to join Jim Shepherd's winning band.

He never had any problems in filling or replacing those members who would not give one hundred percent. His formulae for success was not luck but hard work, practice and dedication - *'We want to win and be the best',* was probably the maxim he instilled into the youngsters which brought almost continuous success.

It was in 1981 that the decision to change the band's name was taken from the South Bradford Music Centre and become Jayess Queensbury Band and was made up from members of the Music Centre band and one or two others who auditioned to be members.

A junior band was flourishing under the title of Jayess Queensbury Junior Band and in later years as Jayess Brass which for some time was led by David Horsfield (Black Dyke cornet player 1966-1973 and had joined Jim as one of the original members of The James Shepherd Versatile Brass in 1973).

Jayess Queensbury Junior Band/Jayess Brass in later years (c: 1992) merged with the former Haworth Band to become known as The Worth Valley Band.

The Jayess Queensbury Band in recent years has benefited from a degree of sponsorship from the West Yorkshire Co-op and as is custom on such occasions the band changed its name to become known as the Jayess (Co-op) Band.

After a short return to the original Jayess Band Jim has now no connection with any of the bands he formed under the Jayess titles. The band has since taken the title of the Yorkshire Co-op (Jayess) Band. In 1998 this band merged with the Jayess 87 Band to become the Yorkshire Co-operatives Band

The Jayess '87 Band was originally another band of youngsters formed by Jim which first met on the 9th of January 1987 in the Wibsey area of Bradford and conducted by Graham Hooper who was the Eb Bass player with Brighouse and Rastrick for many years.

Once it became known that James Shepherd was forming yet another band it was as though he had once again lit the blue touch paper. Youngsters were queuing up to join his band at an alarming rate from as far away as Halifax, Huddersfield, Pudsey and other parts of the Bradford area - the Pied Piper of Bands was at it again.

Initially the band functioned as a youth band just as the original Jayess Band had until 1991 when it too registered in the fourth section to allow it to compete in the Yorkshire Area Championships.

Once again they took the contest by storm and by 1993 had been promoted to the second section.

Continued improvement saw them in the first section of the Yorkshire Area Championships for the first time in 1997 where they took first prize playing Joseph Horovitz's stylish and testing piece 'Ballet for Band'.

This band has so far made three recordings, been on two European concert tours and taken part as the Yorkshire representative at the National Brass Band Champions in London on two occasions and has played host to two visiting bands from Europe. In 1997 they successfully applied for a National Lottery grant and were awarded over £55,000 that will ensure their future. Once again the success of this band has led to yet another offshoot with the Jayess '87 Junior Band.

Although Jim is not connected with this band anymore the band is still going forward and attracting many youngsters to become brass players of the future. Just as all the other bands he has formed over the last thirty years are still doing is a credit to not only his ability but without doubt his standing and the respect he has in the world of brass bands.

Many of the individual members of his bands have gone on to greater musical heights by joining some of the country's leading bands including: The Britannia Building Society Band (now the Fodens (Courtois) Band); British Nuclear Fuels Band (now the JJB Sports Leyland Band); Black Dyke Mills Band; Williams Fairey Band; Grimethorpe Band; Hammonds Sauce Works Band (now the Yorkshire Building Society Band); Yorkshire Imperial Band (now the David Urquart Travel Yorkshire Imperial Band); James Shepherd

Versatile Brass; Desford Colliery Band and the Sellars Engineering Band (now the Sellars International Band).

When this impressive list is joined with such bands as the Life Guards; Scots Guards; Irish Guards; the Ulster Orchestra and the Northern Philharmonia very few individuals can claim to have made such a lasting contribution by introducing so many new players to the brass band movement. Not only to the highest levels of performance but to the movement as a whole where many young people have developed a passion for playing brass band music particularly at a time when many young people are openly criticised these days by many adults for both bad and inconsiderate behaviour.

Whilst his Jayess Queensbury Band were winning one contest after another he still had to produce the goods himself as the leader and driving force behind the James Shepherd Versatile Brass.

On into 1968 when he took the winners prize in the Wind Class of the Teeside International Eisteddfod and achieved the same success in 1970. In the same year he then went on to lead Black Dyke Mills once again to victory in the BBC Band of the Year competition having achieved that distinction previously in 1967. Jim went on to produce a fine performance in the super-charged atmosphere of the King's Hall at Belle Vue when he led Black Dyke to be British Champions playing Gilbert Vinter's 'John O'Gaunt' where once again it was the band's successful partnership with Geoffrey Brand that won that day.

It was in October 1970 under the baton of Geoffrey Brand that he led Black Dyke out onto the Royal Albert Hall stage once again. On that occasion it was to play Frank Wright's arrangement of Berlioz 'Benvenuto Cellini' in what was described as The World Championship and the ultimate prize in the band world. It was however considered by many to be nothing more than a novelty title.

All it seemed to achieve was to give someone else the chance to take the National Championship title.

With that prize going to the Grimethorpe Colliery Band in 1970 and the Wingates Temperance Band in 1971 the brass band movement dabbled with a so-called World Championship but ended up with what seemed inevitable with business as usual. In 1972 when with Geoffrey Brand conducting and Jim in the top chair they took Black Dyke to first place once again playing on this occasion Eric Ball's 'A Kensington Concerto'.

It has often been said that Jim Shepherd, 'The Famous Newbiggin-by-the-Sea Cornet Player', has never forgotten his roots.

This was highlighted in 1971 when he returned to his hometown to help out a local cause when he performed in a concert for the Newbiggin Salvation Army Citadel Organ Fund.

This event would have without doubt brought back his childhood memories of the days when as a young aspiring cornet player he was stepping out to play 'Bless this House' in one of those musical evenings as a guest player at the Newbiggin Salvation Army Citadel. In the audience that night were his parents Florrie and Dickie and sister Florence who would have been three of the proudest people in the world that night.

At this memorable concert he played 'Gentleman Jim' a solo that was specially written for him by John Carr, with the event being sold out weeks in advance the word had gone round that the legend was coming home...

The concert was in aid of the Newbiggin Salvation Army Organ Fund and Jim played that night just for his supper and delighted the packed audience at the Newbiggin Middle School. This was the first time he had been back home to play a solo concert and was described by the audience as a night to remember.

Another special day was on Saturday October 9th, 1971 when he was awarded the Insignia of Honour, which was presented by Peter Wilson the Organising Secretary-Elect of the National Brass Band Championships of Great Britain and National Brass Band Festival.

The following year saw Jim in his last year at Black Dyke and once again leading them to success. Firstly there was the British Open Championship at Belle Vue playing 'Sovereign Heritage' when once again Geoffrey Brand conducted them. This win was to be the first leg of a rare treble at Belle Vue an event that would be seen through 1973 and 1974 by Jim's ultimate successor at Black Dyke, Philip McCann.

Although having led Black Dyke to many successes the 1972 win on Eric Ball's 'A Kensington Concerto' at the Royal Albert Hall was the final curtain on an unprecedented career with the country's leading band but as one door closed another opened. In Jim's case a new career and in some respects an even greater one was about to unfold. Who could have imagined that his next venture with the Versatile Brass would be still pulling in the crowds twenty-five years later.

The concept of the Versatile Brass was said to have been born out of Jim enthusiasm for playing in the Black Dyke Octet. Whilst he liked playing in and rehearsing the Octet almost as much as Black Dyke itself not everyone saw its importance in the same light as he did. Certainly not when it came to how much time should be devoted to rehearsing this eight-man ensemble.

The origins of the Black Dyke Octet date back to 1958 when it was first formed to attend the World Youth Festival in Moscow and following the success of that first outing they were in almost constant demand ever since.

In 1972 a small group under Jim's direction began taking jobs independently from Black Dyke under the title of James Shepherd Versatile Brass. Eventually things came to a head when a meeting was held in the Black Dyke bandroom and Jim was asked the question, 'What's it all about'. Jim stressed that it had not and would not interfere or cause any problems or conflict of interest with his and the other members commitments with Black Dyke and they certainly had no intention of taking any engagements knowing they would clash....

In the end it came down to a straightforward choice either continue playing exclusively with Black Dyke or resign and take up the Versatile Brass full time. Jim decided that having led Black Dyke through one of its most successful periods in its long history it was time to probably move on and continue developing what he had christened, 'The James Shepherd Versatile Brass' into a full time high quality brass ensemble.

The last engagement for Jim at Black Dyke was in the summer of 1973 at Cheltenham Town Hall when he played second man to the band's new principal cornet Philip McCann.

It was after this engagement that David Horsfield, Colin Aspinall and the late Harvey Whiteley also decided to leave and join Jim in his new venture on a more permanent basis.

The original members of the James Shepherd Versatile Brass in 1972 were:

Jim Shepherd (Cornet/Trumpet) *ex-Black Dyke*
David Horsfield (Flugel Horn/Cornet/Trumpet) ex-Black Dyke
Peter Ferris (Trumpet) *ex-Lead trumpeter with Joe Loss Orchestra*
Brian Wood (Horn) *ex-Hammonds*
David Moore (Euphonium) *ex-Grimethorpe*
Derek Southcott (Trombone) *ex-Black Dyke*
Donald Bowes (Bass Trombone) *ex-Hammonds*
Colin Aspinall (Tuba) *ex-Black Dyke*
Harvey Whiteley (Percussion) *ex-Black Dyke*

The group initially met on Sunday's in a room at Outwood near Wakefield. At that first rehearsal they didn't have a conductor, not that they couldn't get one but initially they thought that perhaps they didn't need one.

It was Derek Southcott who first suggested that they should have one. Dennis Wilby a respected man in the band world and David Horsfield's brother-in-law seemed an appropriate choice and was invited to take part in their second rehearsal.

The band's first offical engagement was organised and promoted by themselves and was held in the safe banding territory of Uppermill. Being new and considered by some sceptics as a novelty and unlikely to last the concert turned out to be a resounding success.

Further success followed at Dewsbury and Mansfield, it soon became apparent that this new brass ensemble was of a very high standard and began to attract further bookings throughout the country.

The group's first major break through came when Geoffrey Brand invited them to take part in the massed band gala concert at the Royal Albert Hall following the national finals in 1973. Their part of the programme began with a new work 'Red Skye at Night' which had been written specially for the group by Elgar Howarth and a title given to one of their many disc's in 1981. They concluded their performance with an arrangement written by their conductor Dennis Wilby of Shostakovich's Waltz No.1.

It was without doubt this invitation and the response from the audience that the group's novelty tag, traitors to the true tradition of brass banding, a flash in the pan was finally laid to rest. It saw Jim's dream of putting together a group of musicians who through their special talents, progressiveness and to some extent being a serious novelty in so far as their unique presentation skills being accepted by not only the general public but the brass band movement which ensured the group was to have a rewarding future.

The 1974 line up for one their first L.P's on the Decca label Sounds of Brass series included:

Back Row (left to right) Don Bowes (Second Trombone/Bass Trombone); Stephen Thornton (Cornet/Trumpet); David Moore (Euphonium); Harvey Whiteley (Percussion) and John Pollard (Solo Trombone)
Middle Row: David Hirst (Cornet/Trumpet); Gordon Higginbottom (Tenor Horn) Colin Aspinall (Eb Bass);
Front Row: David Horsfield (Cornet/Flugel horn); Dennis Wilby (Conductor) and James Shepherd (Cornet/Trumpet)

The group went on to be invited to perform at the Royal Albert Hall again in 1976 and 1979. The second visit to the Royal Albert Hall is without doubt one of Jim's most memorable musical moments when the audience were determined to keep them on stage and the satisfaction that the group had finally been accepted.

The audience went wild with programmes thrown in the air and a standing ovation as well, so much so that the Massed Bands had to wait in the wings until they finally came off stage.

One particular performance with the Versatile Brass which called for Jim to be ice cool and have nerves of steel was on the occasion when the group was asked to perform at the Berlin Philharmonic Hall in front of a capacity audience.

Not only was the concert hall pack but it was heard live on German national radio and also went out live on the B.B.C's Friday Night is Music Night radio programme. Playing the old favourite 'Pandora' it was said to have been one of Jim's finest solo performances under what could only be described as the ultimate in pressure

Throughout the 1970's and 1980's and between an ever growing list of engagements both home and abroad for his Versatile Brass the young people who he moulded into the Jayess Bands were having what could only be described as unrivalled success in everything they did.

Even during these hectic times he still found time to help his old friend Geoff Whitham out at his Hammond Sauce Works Band by joining them for the 1974 Granada Band of the year competition.

In 1977 and 1978 he was back in the North East playing with the Ever Ready Band the former Craghead Colliery and was featured on a couple of L.P records they produced during those two years.

Every year at the British Open Championship the presentation of the Iles Medal on behalf of the Worshipful Company of Musicians takes place. It was John Henry Iles who gave his name to this medal, a man who achieved so much for the brass band movement during his lifetime.

On behalf of the Company the Iles Medal has been presented annually to some of the most notable names in the brass band world. These have included the three Mortimer brothers, Harry, Alex and Rex, along with father and son John R. and Dennis Carr. Other notable recipients have included Eric Ball, Stanley Boddington, Dennis Wright, Frank Wright, Thomas J. Powell, Drake Rimmer, William Wood, Leonard Lamb, George Thompson, Walter Hargreaves, Albert Coupe and in 1989 James Shepherd joined this distinguished group.

To receive recognition in this way and to be associated and talked of in the same breath as these giants of the band world is certainly an honour indeed.

In 1993 after twenty-five years he took a two-year break from the Versatile Brass as a planned moved to retire from top class playing.

Throughout this period he was kept busy as the group's Chairman. In 1996 he was back - you can't hold a good man down - he re-joined not only as Chairman but back as a full time playing member.

In 1997 he finally retired from the James Shepherd Versatile Brass and now the ensemble have changed the name just to The Versatile Brass.

Over the last few years Jim's life has almost come round full circle when he was invited to become Newbiggin Band's professional conductor.

In 1996 the band that gave him his start all those years ago had found a new and much welcomed sponsor and following the usual tradition in banding circles on these occasions were re-named the Greggs Bakery Band (Newbiggin Band).

The Greggs Bakery Brass Band - June 1997

Once again success was not far off when he conducted them into the prizes at the 1996-second section C.I.S.W.O. contest at Blackpool playing Goff Richards 'Hollywood', when they were awarded a second prize. Although not winning a prize he led the band to a creditable 8th place in the 1997-second section National Finals in Birmingham.

In 1998 they were once again in the prizes qualifying for the 1998-second section National Finals, which were held in Harrogate and going on to repeat that success in 1999 by winning the first section area contest playing Arthur Bliss's test piece 'Kenilworth'. A piece that the great pre-war Foden's Motor Works Band had first played to great success under their legendary conductor Fred Mortimer at the last Crystal Palace when they took the first prize at the National Brass Band Championships of 1936.

Working very closely with the band's musical director David Binding Greggs Bakery Band hope for even greater success when they join the Championship section next year.

He is still delighting audiences with his skill and brilliance in concert halls, guest appearances and in more recent times and to use banding jargon as the third man down in the highly successful film 'Brassed Off'.

He has been involved in countless radio and television programmes both as a soloist and during his time as a principal cornet player. He has been involved in the recording of many records dating back to his first 45 r.p.m. in 1963 at Black Dyke Mills under the baton of Jack Emmott when the solo he played was Edrich Siebert's 'The Lazy Trumpeter', which was recorded two weeks after he joined the band.

Although they got his name right on the disc the record producers used the wrong photograph on the record sleeve which still showed Maurice Murphy as the principal cornet player with the band.

This was only an error because being the brand new principal cornet player there was no new photograph available for the record sleeve.

In 1994 he was also invited to take his rightful place amongst the giants of the band world who performed and produced the 'Kings of Brass' compact disc.

The Dream Team

The 1994 Solo Cornet line up for the first Kings of Brass recording 'Down Memory Lane'
(Left to right): Peter Read; Derek Garside; James Shepherd; David Read and Tony Whitaker.

In 1997 on his latest compact disc 'Gentleman Jim' he shares the spotlight on two of the tracks with his daughter Claire who was the former Principal Cornet player with Yorkshire Co-op (Jayess) Band and former Flugel player with Sellars Engineering Band. She is now the Principal Cornet player at Glossop Old and led them in the 1998 Championship Section.

Jim's daughter Helen did play in Jayess Junior band for a short while but has since retired and James Shepherd Jnr, whilst appreciating his father's achievements chose not to follow in his father footsteps.

It is now almost fifty years since James Shepherd took those first tentative lessons under the guiding hand and watchful eye of his father. From that day on few individuals have contributed so much to the brass band movement as he has done.

Many years ago relatives in the United States of America wrote and sent this poem dedicated it to their nephew:

The Man Who Wins

If you think you are beaten - you are,
If you think you dare not - you don't,
If you would like to win, but think you can't
It is almost certain that you won't.

Life's battles don't always go,
To the strongest or fastest man
But sooner or later, the one who wins
Is the man who thinks he can.......

...and finally... whilst some people may call him an ambassador for the brass band movement and some others may see him as a role model for young up and coming musicians. What ever is said of him the one thing we can all say is that James Shepherd is a winner and a true legend in the world of brass bands. The tributes at the end of this story are from some of the most respected musicians in the brass band movement and their contribution is a testament to James Shepherd.

Recordings

1. Black Dyke Mills Band

a) Black Dyke Mills Band – 1963 – EMI (7EG8818).

b) Black Dyke Mills Band – 1964 – EMI (CLP1787)

c) Carnival of Venice – 1966 – Hallmark (HMA211)

d) The Virtuoso band – 1966 – Golden Guinea (SGL10391)

e) Yellow Submarine/Thingumybob – 1966 – Apple (APPLE 4)

f) With Band and Voices – 1968 – Pye (NSPL18209)

g) A Christmas Festival – 1968 – Pye (NSPL18259)

h) The Trumpets – 1968 – Pye (NSPL18265)

i) Championship Brass Series – 1968 – Paxton (LPT1027)

j) Championship Brass series - 1969 – Paxton (LPT1028)

k) The Champions – 1968 – Pye (GSGL10410)

l) Champions Again – 1969 – Pye Top Brass (GGL0427)

m) Black Dyke in Concert – 1969 – Golden Guinea (GGL0417)

n) Massed Band Concert Royal Albert Hall – 1969 – Pye (GSGL10445)

o) High Peak for Brass – 1970 – Pye Top Brass (GSGL10453)

p) Ivory and Brass – 1970 – Golden Guinea (GSGL10463)

q) Handel's Messiah – 1971 – Pye (GSGL10475)

r) World Champion Brass – 1971 – Golden Guinea (GSGL10477)

s) Triumphant Brass – 1972 – Pye Top Brass (GSGL10489)

t) Brass to the Fore – 1972 – RCA (LSA3088)

u) Black Dyke Double Champions - Sounding Brass Series Vol.8 - 1973 – Decca (SB308)

2. 'The Virtuosi Band'.

He was the Principal Cornet player on almost all of their nine recordings between 1973/77.

3. Solo Brass No.1

a) Keith Swallow accompanying on piano–1972-KennedyRecording Company (KRCSB1)

4. James Shepherd plays Popular Contrasts – 1982 – Look ((LK/LP7000)

5. James Shepherd '3Valves & 88 Keys" – Date not known – Fanfare (MS65)

6. James Shepherd Versatile Brass.

a) James Shepherd Versatile Brass – 1973 – Kennedy KRC (VB1/KRCSB2)

b) Sounds of Brass Series Vol. 14 - 1974 – Decca (SB314)

c) Sounds of Brass Series Vol. 21 – 1975 – Decca (SB321)

d) The James Shepherd Versatile Brass – 1975 – Varagram (ET40)

e) National Brass Band Concert – 1973 – Decca (SKL5171)

f) National Brass Band Concert – 1976 – RCA (LSA3285)

g Whole in One – 1977 – VBDC (VBDC1)

h) Cornet Carillon / To a Wild Rose - 1978 - Look (LK/SP6368A – B)

i) Sounds of Brass – 1978 - Decca (SB331)

j) J.S.V.B with Colne Valley Male Voice Choir – 1978 – Look (LK/LP6043)

k) National Brass Band Concert – 1979 – Chandos Brass Band Series (BBR1003)

l) Strike up the Band – 1979 - Sounds of Brass series – Decca (SB337)

m) Ten of the Best – 1980 – Look (LK/LP6467)

n) Red Skye at Night – 1981 – Look (LK/LP6600)

o) Simply Versatile – 1983 – Polyphonic (PRL019)

p) Rhythm and Blues – 1987 – Polyphonic (PRL035D)

q) Brassmen's Holiday – 1988 – Versatile Brass/Brass Service, (Martigny, Switzerland (JSVB100)

7. Stars in Brass – 1987 – Peter Nicholas, Redacre Records Vol.1 (PN1)

8. Ever Ready Band - Sounds of Brass Series – 1977 – Decca (SB329)

9. Ever Ready Band - Sounds of Brass Series - 1978 – Decca (SB334)

10. Ireland Alloys Band

a) James Shepherd plays Rule Britannia – 1978 - Symbol Records (LL735)

11. The National Brass Band - Golden Melodies – 1980 – K.Tel (ONE 1075)

12. The Jayess (Queensbury) Band - 'Making Tracks Number 1' 1983

13. The Jayess (Queensbury) Band - 'Making Tracks Number 2' 1985

14. The Jayess (Queensbury) Band -'Making Tracks Number 3' 1987– C.J.S.Recording

15. Sounds like Christmas - The Jayess (Queensbury) Band – 1988 – (JSLP105)

16. 'Down Memory Lane' - Kings of Brass CD – 1995 – Kirklees Music (KRCD1019)

17. Gentleman Jim CD - 1997 - Kirklees Music (KRCD1028)

18. 'Down Memory Lane' Kings of Brass - 2 CD - 1997 - Kirklees Music (KRCD1029)

(Numbers 16,17,18 and number 2 in a compilation from the nine Virtuosi Band recordings are still available from Kirklees Music (01484 –722855)

Over the years Jim Shepherd has been heard on countless recordings, whilst the above list highlights just how many recordings I have been able to find where he has performed both as a soloist and/or as a member of a band I have no doubt there will be some that I have missed.

TRIBUTES

I have known Jim since 1962 when he came to help Black Dyke on some engagements and was eventually persuaded to join full time in May 1963 when his first engagement was my last as a player. This was in the middle of his 'hat trick' of wins at the prestigious British Solo Championships.

Throughout the long number of years I have been involved in the brass band movement I can say that Jim is the most accurate cornetist of all time, his articulation and production of sound is second to none.

I am pleased to have been asked to contribute these few words to this book and feel that many individuals from the world of brass bands have long since been forgotten over the years. I certainly hope this book and others similar publications I know Chris Helme has in the pipeline will be successful because they will to remind us all of just a few of the personalities from our world of brass bands.

Geoffrey Whitham – former Principal Euphonium Black Dyke Mills Band; Musical Director Hammond Sauce Works Band; Conductor; Teacher; Adjudictor and a friend of long standing.

Re-calling Jim Shepherd is to be reminded and to 're-hear' a stream of golden cornet tone, which never fails to provoke feelings of sheer pleasure and joy. Quality brings its own special message. My years during the late 1960's and early 70's as Professional Conductor of Black Dyke Mills Band meant that I enjoyed regular contact with many fine instrumentalists all of who were dedicated to musical excellence. In the pursuit of a golden sound, none was more 'golden' than Jim.

Whether in the bandroom (I cannot re-call Jim ever missing a rehearsal), concerts or contests his technique and control never faltered. Jim Shepherd is an artist of the cornet, an accolade justified by very few.

As the principal cornetist Jim was featured as a soloist on most Black Dyke Mills Band concerts. His many recordings bear testimony to a remarkable ability. Listen to his triple tonguing – a model of even articulation; his quality of sound over the whole range; his spacing – so that the music never sounds hurried or pushed along; his ease of performance so that one forgets the technical feats being encompassed. I could go on; the recordings – available for all to enjoy – say it all.

Alongside his musical qualities Jim Shepherd exudes a natural modesty, always willing to offer his knowledge and experience, courteously, sincerely and generously.

It remains a special satisfaction to have shared years of musical endeavour, which has been enriched by a friendship built on admiration and respect. Thank you, Jim, for it all.

Geoffrey Brand ARAM, LRAM, ARCM.
Professional Conductor Black Dyke Mills Band (1967 – 1974)

In my opinion Jim Shepherd is the finest cornet player within my living memory. Jim's contribution to the success of the Black Dyke Mills Band of the 1960's and 70's is testament to his skill, not only as a player, but also as a first class musician and leader of the Band. Jim's skill as a player was never in doubt, but he also had the ability to motivate everyone who came into contact with him, imparting his vast experience and enthusiasm on all.

David Hirst MA.,BEd (Hons),LTCL,Cert Ed – Soprano Cornet Black Dyke Mills Band; James Shepherd Versatile Brass; teacher, adjudicator and currently the Resident Conductor at Brighouse and Rastrick Band.

I never heard Jimmy play whilst he was at Black Dyke but I heard a lot about him, by then I had gone to the Halle Orchestra. I had a friend who played me some records of him and I thought they were marvellous. After hearing them I thought no one else could be better, they were beautifully played. Whilst I was at the Halle Orchestra we had a recording contract which specified only one microphone, the engineer Bob Auger who became a good friend was also involved in some Black Dyke Mills Band recordings and told me what a great player Jimmy Shepherd was and about his Versatile Brass group who were great.

The first time I met Jimmy in person was in Wales, he had the job of training the Welsh Youth Brass Band and whilst he looked after the top cornets I took the second cornets. I recall taking a walk with him one afternoon and we found a small music shop with some Vincent Bach mouthpieces in the window, priced £5, we both bought one and I still have mine.

I recall having had the pleasure of playing along side him at the Free Trade Hall in Manchester. What I admired in him was his modesty and his kindness and in my opinion he'll certainly take some beating.

Bill Lang – Principal Cornet -Black Dyke Mills Band; Principal Trumpet - The Halle Orchestra; Principal Trumpet – The London Symphony Orchestra

There are few words to describe the admiration I have for James Shepherd. He inspired me as a young cornet player with his beautiful tone and immaculate technique.

I first met him as a young lad of fourteen when I was competing in the National Solo Championships of Great Brtiain in 1966. He had completed his hat trick in 1965 and was present as a guest of honour.

I was terribly nervous to be playing in this competition in such celebrated company, James Shepherd came over to me before the contest started and gave me much confidence and words of advice. This helped me enormously to settle down and play to my potential. I was lucky enough to win that day, but I have always been grateful to Jim for those few encouraging words.

His dedication to his art and generosity of spirit, make him one of those very special people who come into ones life so rarely and fleetingly.

The work Jim has done so selflessly in the field of education is quite priceless and his legacy will live on for many generations.

In 1988, I was conducting the National Youth Band of Wales and the tutors were asked to form a brass quintet to entertain the students after a particularly hard day rehearsing, I had the immense thrill of sitting next to Jim Shepherd in a brass quintet, which will remain one of the high spots of my career.

James Watson FRAM., FLCM Artistic Director – former Principal Cornet Desford Colliery Band; former Principal Trumpet Royal Philharmonic Orchestra, London Sinfonietta and the Royal Opera House; Professor of Trumpet Royal College of Music and the Professional Conductor Black Dyke Band.

Having been invited to write some words as a tribute to one of the truly great personalities of the brass band movement is a privilege, but when that person has also been not merely a working colleague, but friend, makes the task even more pleasurable.

Jim Shepherd and I go back more years than possibly either of us would like to remember. Strangely enough one of my first recollections of being in Jim's "company" was on a football field in Aldershot. He and I were both doing our National Service in the Army, Jim serving with the Staff Band of the Royal Army Medical Corps, whilst I was with the Staff Band of the Royal Army Service Corps. The various bands in the Aldershot District ran a Band Football League and being members of our respective bands football teams, we met regularly on the field of play, plus musically coming into contact during the many massed bands engagements.

It was some years after de-mob that Jim and I were re-united. Living at the time in Ireland, I travelled to attend Dyke's rehearsals and their appearance at the National Brass Band

Championships of 1967 ("Journey into Freedom"). What a wonderful musical experience that was, and I still rate their performance with Geoffrey Brand conducting as one of the all-time greats.

Jim and I eventually became working colleagues for the West Riding Education Authority as Peripatetic Brass Tutors and it was during this period that he had a vision to form a 10-piece brass group. He used the very best players of the day and introduced audiences to a completely new style of music. He invited me to become the group's first Musical Director…James Shepherd Versatile Brass was born.

The formation of the group caused chaos in many Yorkshire top bands during the ensuing month's, as players involved in this venture left their respective bands due to the sheer volume of interest in Jim's brilliant new vision.

The early pioneering days of Versatile Brass were both challenging and rewarding as the group established their unique repertoire and at the same time a full diary. This included an early appearance as guest artists at The National Brass Band Festival Concert in the Royal Albert Hall - a highlight of those early days. They were some of the most exciting memories and Jim's vision in the following years was to prove highly desirable, and as the saying goes…the rest is history.

Dyke have been blessed with many illustrious names occupying that famous "end chair", but none were more dedicated or successful that the gentleman in question. Jim was a fine leader and will go down in history as one of the truly great principal solo cornets of this famous Yorkshire band. It was a privilege and honour working with him and also being a friend.

Dennis Wilby – Adjudicator; Conductor; Composer/Arranger; Editor of Brass Review and the first Musical Director of the James Shepherd Versatile Brass.

I first met Jim Shepherd in the early 1960's; my initial impressions were of a warm personality and a brilliant soloist. Little did I know at the time that I would be privileged to be a colleague of his, firstly in Black Dyke and then in the original James Shepherd Versatile Brass ensemble for 18 years.

During that time there were many memorable performances from him, none more so than in the Philharmonic Hall, Berlin when his playing left the audience (and his colleagues) spellbound.

In recent years he has played with the 'Kings of Brass' and showed that he still has that magic – truly a legend of the cornet.

David W.Horsfield – former Brighouse and Rastrick Band and Black Dyke Mills Band; original member James Shepherd Versatile Brass; member of the Kings of Brass; Adjudicator; Conductor and music publisher.

From the first rehearsal at Carlton Main Frickley Colliery Band you knew he was going to be someone special. His technique and fullness of sound throughout the range of the cornet left you in no doubt of his ability.

A quite humble person, certainly not conceited at all, he just let his musicianship and artistry of his controlled cornet playing do the talking for him.

He has a warm, inspiring personality and over many years he has endeavoured to pass his expertise on to many young players through the many bands he has both started and been involved with. He is known to many as "Gentleman Jim" and who could argue with that…

Barry Thompson – former member of the Carlton Main Frickley Colliery Band and Grimethorpe Colliery Band; Adjudicator; Teacher and Conductor.

I can remember during the very 1960's giving Jim a lift in my car after he appeared for the first time with Black Dyke as a guest principal at Cliffe Castle in Keighley after Maurice Murphy had left. It was on the journey home that Jim expressed some doubts about joining Black Dyke as he felt the band's sound was too large for him to penetrate through. However, after some persuasion he did join and the rest as they say is history. I myself feel very privileged to have been a member of the winning quartet at the Oxford Solo and Quartet Championships in 1964 the same year that Jim won the national soloist first prize for the third consecutive time. A player of great accuracy, I rarely heard him play a mistake during his solo performances with the band.

John H.Clay B.A.(Hons) - former member Black Dyke Mills Band (1959 – 1975) and Conductor.

I am glad that my time working with brass bands has coincided with the career of James Shepherd, certainly on of the finest and most enjoyable cornet players I have ever heard. Throughout my playing and conducting days in Scotland, I often heard James perform as soloist. He was and indeed still is an inspiration – musical, sensitive, secure and a player of great personality.

In the early seventies, when I was responsible for the National Brass Band Championships, I had the opportunity to get to know him on a personal level, I found that the warmth and dependability evidenced in his playing was part of the character of the man.

In later years, as a publisher, I have worked with James at various times and have found that added to his many musical attributes, there is an engaging modesty, which singles him out as a very special person.

That he is still playing, conducting and bringing his influence to bear on the band scene is confirmation of his interest in brass bands – without him we would be the poorer.

Peter Wilson – Managing Editor, 'British Bandsman'.

James Shepherd (though he will always be Jim to me and to many other admirers) followed a line of famous star cornet players into the hottest seat in banding - the 'end chair' of Black Dyke Mills Band. Amongst his predecessors were John Paley, Ceres Jackson, Harold Pinches, Harold Jackson, Owen Bottomley and of course, still with us Willie Lang and Maurice Murphy. To follow what to many was a 'royal line of succession' must have been, to say the least, daunting. That Jim did it, and did it with distinction, is unquestionable.

For ten years he held the position, serving under professional conductors, Colonel C.H.Jaeger and Geoffrey Brand and alongside bandmasters Jack Emmott, Geoffrey Whitham and myself. During these years Jim helped the band win the British Open titles at the Belle Vue September contest in 1968 and 1972, National Titles at the Royal Albert Hall in 1967 and 1972 and the World Championships at the same venue in 1972. In his last full year, the band achieved the distinction of becoming double champions winning both British Open and National titles - a rare achievement indeed.

With the band fulfilling 60 to 70 concerts per year and in virtually all of them Jim played at least one stand-up solo. Amongst his favourites were Naploi, Cleopatra and Pandora, audiences were treated to flawless performances of these and others time after time.

This was in addition to fulfilling the duties of 'leader', in which he was of the variety affectionately known as 'work–horses', meaning that he was not one of those who merely played the 'tasty' bits – he also pulled his weight with the heavy stuff.

They were memorable times, and it was a matter of great regret when, in 1973, Jim announced his retirement from the band to devote his full attention to the already highly successful James Shepherd Versatile Brass. This ensemble broke new ground in brass entertainment and quickly attained a world-wide reputation with its modern arrangements, slick presentation and its own individual brand of humour.

Even this was just another part of the story - as Jim built a reputation as one of the finest teachers, even forming bands from his pupils, passing on to them his expertise and experience leading on to another extension of his work with bands - conducting in which he continues to notch up notable successes.

Despite all this, it is as one of the greatest cornet players of our time that James Shepherd will be remembered. Even now, over a quarter of a century since his departure from Black Dyke, he can still turn on the magic. I know - I experienced it in a concert only recently.

Roy Newsome B.Mus., FRCO, ARCM - former Resident Conductor Black Dyke Mills Band; Conductor; Adjudicator; Composer and Arranger.

...coda... I over heard two small girls who had taken part in the under 11 section at the 1999 Annual Elland Silver Band Slow Melody competition talking to each other just before the results were to be announced when one said to her friend in a very serious tone,

'... I bet you wouldn't win if Jim Shepherd were in it....'

...a LEGEND indeed, now what price do you place on this level of acclaim...

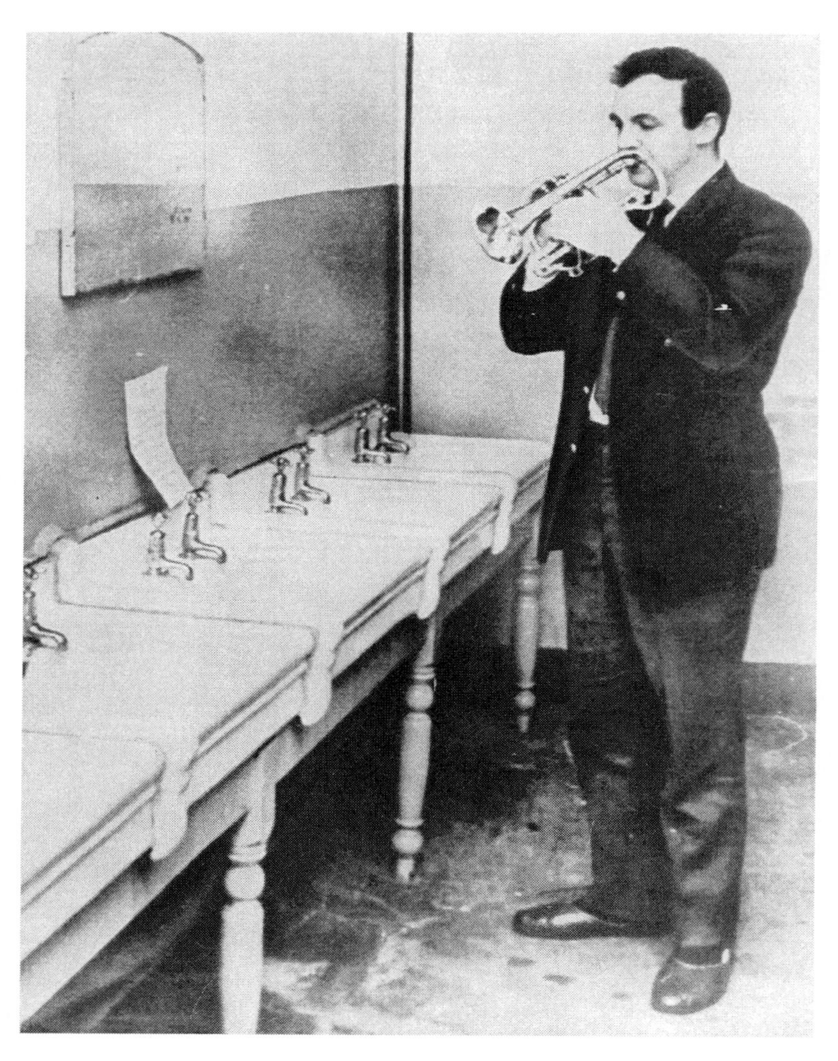

A little bit of last minute rehearsal – 'practice makes perfect' – even wearing your carpet slippers.

THE AUTHOR

Chris Helme has lived all his life in Brighouse, a small West Yorkshire town and a community that is perhaps better known to the wider audience for the exploits of its famous brass band, the Brighouse and Rastrick Band.

He was educated locally and in 1970 joined the police service with postings in both Leeds and Bradford. Since 1975 he has been stationed principally in his hometown of Brighouse. Firstly, as the Community Constable in the district he grew up in as a child, a role that lasted for almost 16 years. Now, after almost twenty-eight years and coming to the end of his service he is the Crime Prevention Officer for the Brighouse and Elland areas. In 1990 he was awarded the British Empire Medal for his service to his community.

His introduction to brass bands came in 1960 when a neighbour invited him to a rehearsal at the Clifton and Lightcliffe Band. Taking lessons from two respected stalwarts of the band he progressed from playing a Cornet to the Flugel Horn and even aspired to being invited for an audition at the famous Brighouse and Rastrick Band.... but, now finally after waiting thirty-five years he has long since resigned himself to the fact he is not going to hear from them again but it was still nice to be asked. Having played with Clifton and Lightcliffe, West Yorkshire Police Band and a short spell with the Elland Silver Band he is now on his second spell playing the Eb flat bass with the West Yorkshire Police Band.

His interest in local history began in 1975 whilst serving as a Community Constable and in 1986 published his first local history book with a second two years later followed by a number of other publications. Over the years he has written a number of articles for both local, national magazines and for the last fourteen years a weekly nostalgia column for the Brighouse Echo. He is in regular demand to give lectures and presentations to all kinds of groups in the West Yorkshire area including many local Junior Schools.

He has produced this book by combining his brass band knowledge and researching skills and it is hoped will only be the first and form part of a continuing series of similar publications. It is hoped that it will help us all to appreciate and remember some of those people both past and present that have possessed an exceptional talent and have all gone on to make a significant contribution to the brass band movement over many years.

When all their records are almost too scratched to play any more and may be the only place left to buy them from are the second hand or charity shops. Or their C D's are reduced to the deletions list, what is there left to remind us of those people that this movement can quite rightly describe as 'Legends', those select few people who have or can inspire us all to perhaps try just a little harder.

 - Tower House, Holme Mews, Wakefield Road, Lightcliffe, Halifax HX3 8TY - 01422-205763